EPIC SPACE ADVENTURE

MARS
ROVER
RESCUE

ANDREW RADER

ILLUSTRATIONS BY GALEN FRAZER

MEET THE CREW:

Name: MC Longneck
Occupation: Explorer
Favorite food: Pizza
"Let's see what's out there"

Name: Dr. Xia
Occupation: Scientist
Favorite food: Bamboo smoothie
"Follow the data"

Name: Sputnik
Occupation: Mechanic
Favorite food: Electrons
"Beep-boop-beep"

Name: Mira
Occupation: Pilot
Favorite food: Peanuts
"Start the engines"

Name: Jake
Occupation: Engineer
Favorite food: Carrots
"Problem... solved"

Name: Rover ("Trailblazer")
Occupation: Scout
Favorite food: Plutonium-238
"Rrrrr"

A signal from Earth. A beep and a blip. Cruising through space, we're recalled from our trip.

Back past the planets,
to Earth we fly.

Our ship is racing home,
but we don't know why.

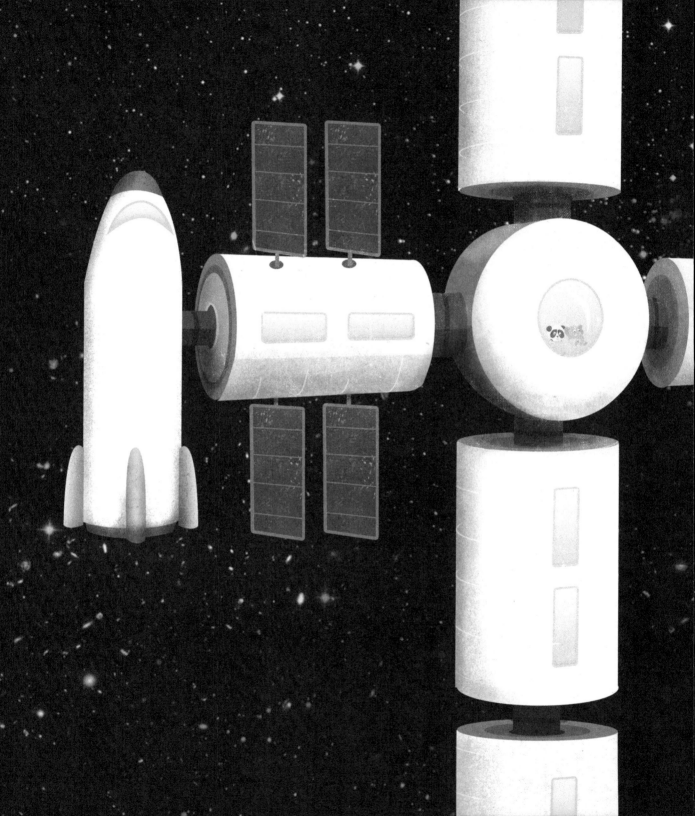

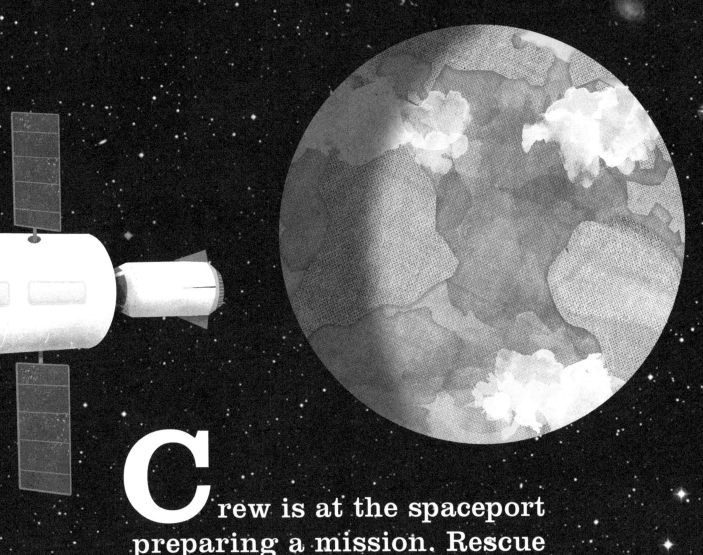

Crew is at the spaceport preparing a mission. Rescue on Mars?

"We've received a transmission."

D
r. Xia is leading a search for a rover that's lost.

"It crashed on Mars, and must be found at all cost!"

Everyone needs to train for the journey ahead.

"Time to exercise—no more sleeping in bed!"

Fueling
the ship,
almost ready
to go.

Loading supplies—
"Careful with that cargo!"

Get into the cockpit and buckle up tight.

"Start up the engines:
3...2...1...Light!"

High above
Earth, we're
among the stars.

"Navigator—set the ship
on a course for Mars!"

EARTH

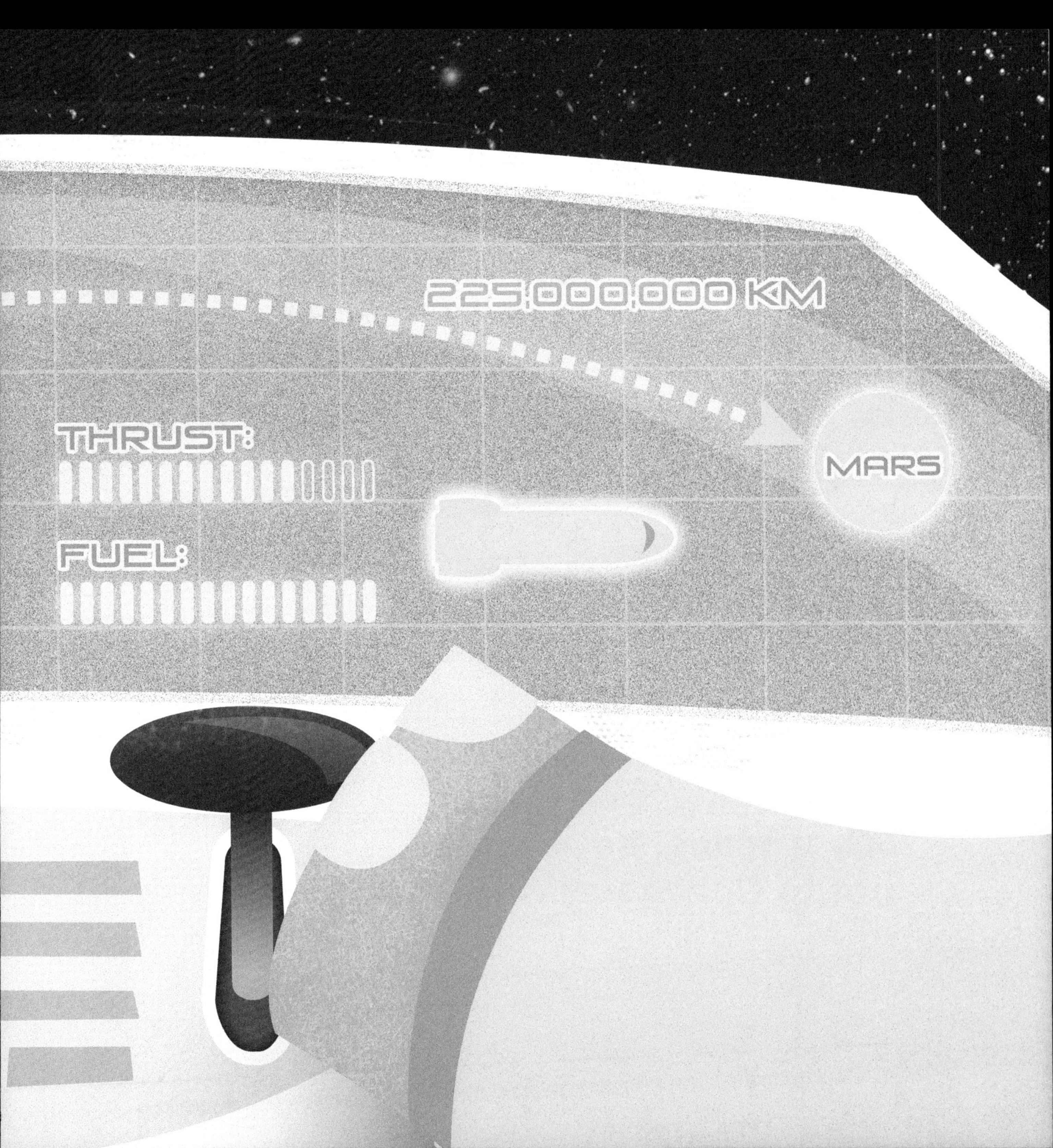
225,000,000 KM
THRUST:
FUEL:
MARS

In space, be careful not to float away.

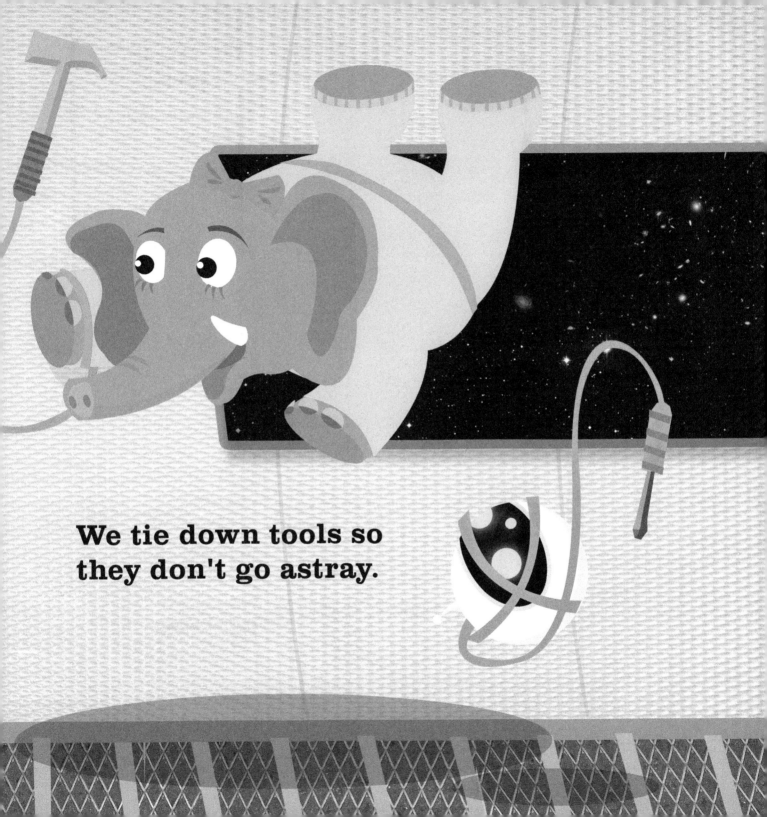

We tie down tools so
they don't go astray.

"**J**oin me in the cockpit,
we'll be there soon."

"Start the
landing,
and watch out
for that moon!"

Keep the ship steady as
we land in place—on the surface
of Mars, right next to our base.

"**L**et's settle in and gather supplies. We'll start the search at tomorrow's sunrise."

M elt ice to get water, and grow some food.

Hope you like potatoes fried,
baked, and stewed.

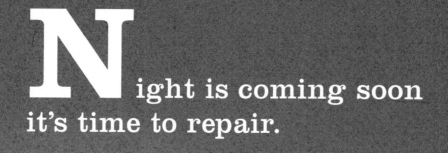

Night is coming soon
it's time to repair.

Mend that hole in the base,
it's leaking out air!

Outside
Mars is cold,
but we're warm
and snug.

Sipping milk and cocoa
that's steaming your mug.

P

reparing to search,
we wake up at dawn.

"Pack up your gear and put your space suit on."

Quickly eat breakfast and pile into the truck.

Let's search for the rover, and hope for some luck.

Roll out for the mission, over the sand.

Can we find a lost rover
across all of this land?

S
earching
all over, which
way should
we go?

"Towards the volcano, along the old lava flow."

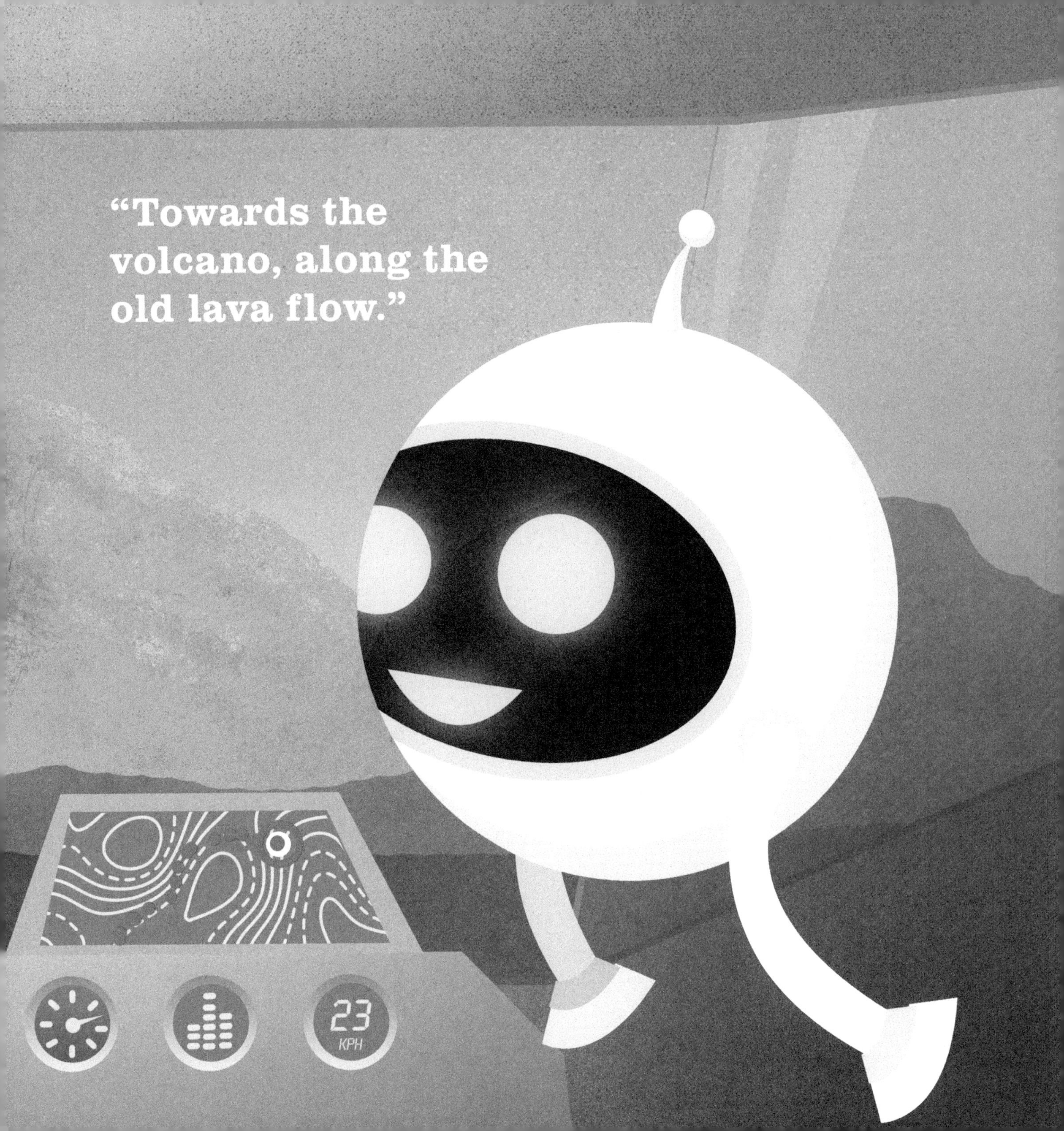

Through the deep canyon,
we get help on our quest.

Detecting a beacon—"We need
to head west!"

U

nder the sand dune,
what do we see?

A piece of the rover,
buried deep as could be.

Vigorous
digging, the
rover is free.

"Is there any
damage?
Let's look
and see."

Wheels are OK, but the computer won't start.

Clean out the dust, and replace that spare part.

X-country
we drive back in
our Martian truck.

"Oh no,
engine trouble,
what—are
we stuck?"

Yanking and tugging to
our destination—that brave little
rover pulled us back to the station!

Zero regrets,
that mission
was great!

That's what
happens when
you cooperate.

IF YOU LOVED MARS ROVER RESCUE...

READ...MC LONGNECK'S

EPIC
SPACE
ADVENTURE

THE CREATORS:

Andrew Rader is an aerospace engineer, author, and game designer from Canada but based at SpaceX in Los Angeles. He's an avid trivia player, space and Mars enthusiast, science nerd, history buff, and incurable know-it-all.

Galen Frazer is a graphic artist and self-proclaimed space geek based in the Baltimore area. When not illustrating totally rad space books, he enjoys spending time with his family and playing guitar.

For information regarding permission, write to the publisher, StoryBook Genius, at:
4171 Crescent Dr., Ste. 101-A, St. Louis, MO 63129 or visit them on the Internet at
www.sbgpublishing.com
ISBN 978-1-941434-56-7

StoryBook Genius
Publishing

Publishing
Brilliantly
Illustrated
Children's Books

www.sbgpublishing.com

CPSIA information can be obtained
at www.ICGtesting.com
Printed in the USA
BVOW05s0217221117

501074BV00016B/214/P